This is George.

He lived with his friend, the man with the yellow hat.

He was a good little monkey and always very curious.

This morning George was curious the moment he woke
up because he knew it was a special day . . .

At breakfast George's friend said: "Today we are going to celebrate because just three years ago this day I brought you home with me from the jungle. So tonight I'll take you to the animal show. But first I have a surprise for you."

H. A. REY

Curious George
rides a bike

Houghton Mifflin Company, Boston

Rides A Bike

LIBRARY OF CONGRESS CATALOG CARD NUMBER 52-8728
ISBN: 0-395-16964-X (rnf.)
ISBN: 0-395-17444-9 (pbk.)

Printed in the United States of America

WOZ   Thirty-Second Printing

He took George out to the yard where a big box was standing. George was very curious.

Out of the box came a bicycle. George was delighted; that's what he had always wanted. He knew how to ride a bicycle but he had never had one of his own.

"I must go now," said the man, "but I'll be back in time for the show. Be careful with your new bike and keep close to the house while I am gone!"

George could ride very well. He could even do
all sorts of tricks (monkeys are good at that).

For instance he could ride this way,
with both hands off the handle bar,

and he could ride this way,

like a cowboy on a wild bronco,

and he could also ride backwards.

But after a while George got tired of doing tricks and

went out into the street. The newsboy was just passing by with his bag full of papers. "It's a fine bike you have there," he said to George. "How would you like to help me deliver the papers?"

He handed George the bag and told him to do one
side of the street first and
then turn back and
do the other side.

George was very
proud as he rode off
with his bag.

12

He started to
deliver the papers
on one side of the street
as he had been told.

When he came to the last house
he saw a little river in the distance.

George was curious: he wanted to know
what the river was like, so instead of turning back
to deliver the rest of the papers he just went on.

There was a lot to see at the river:

a man was fishing from the bridge,

a duck family was paddling downstream,

and two boys were playing with their boats.

George would have liked to stop and look at the boats,

but he was afraid the boys might find out that he had not

delivered all the papers. So he rode on.

While riding along George kept thinking of boats all
the time. It would be such fun to have a boat — but how could
he get one? He thought and thought — and then he had an idea.

He got off the bicycle, took a newspaper out of the bag
and began to fold it.

First he folded down the corners, like this,

| then he folded both edges up, | brought the ends together | and flattened it sidewise. |

| Then he turned one corner up, | then the other one, | again brought the ends together |

| and flattened it sidewise. | Then, gently, he pulled the ends open — |

and there was his BOAT!

Now the moment had come to launch the boat. Would it float?   It did!

So George decided to make some more boats. Finally he had used up all the papers and had made so many boats that he could not count them — a whole fleet.

Watching his fleet

sailing down the river

George felt like an admiral.

But watching his fleet he forgot to watch where he was going —

suddenly there was a terrible jolt: the bicycle had hit a rock
and George flew off the seat, head first.

Luckily George was not hurt, but the front wheel of the bicycle was all out of shape and the tire was blown out.

George tried to ride the bicycle, but of course it wouldn't go.

So he started carrying it, but it soon got too heavy.

George did not know WHAT to do: his new bike was

spoiled, the newspapers were gone. He wished he had listened to his friend and kept close to the house. Now he just stood there and cried . . .

Suddenly his face brightened. Why — he had forgotten that he could ride on one wheel! He tried it and it worked. He had hardly started out again when he saw something

he had never seen before: rolling toward him came an enormous tractor with huge trailers behind it. Looking out

of the trailers were all sorts of animals. To George it
looked like a Zoo on wheels. The tractor stopped and two

men jumped out. "Well, well,"
said one of the men, "a little
monkey who can ride a bike
bronco fashion! We can use you
in our animal show tonight.
I am the director of the show
and this is Bob.

He can straighten your wheel
and fix that flat in no time
and then we'll take you
along to the place
where the show
is going to be."

So the three of them got into the cab and drove off.
"Maybe you could play a fanfare while you ride your bike in
the show," the director said. "I have a bugle for you right
here, and later on you'll get a green coat and a cap just like
Bob's."

On the show grounds everybody was busy getting things ready for the show. "I must do some work now," said the director. "Meanwhile you may have a look around and

get acquainted with all the animals — but you must not feed them, especially the ostrich because he will eat anything and might get very sick afterwards."

31

George was curious: would the ostrich really eat anything? He wouldn't eat a bugle—or would he? George went a little closer to the cage — and before he knew it

the ostrich had snatched the bugle and tried to swallow it.
But a bugle is hard to swallow, even for an ostrich; it got
stuck in his throat. Funny
sounds came out of the bugle
as the ostrich was struggling with
it, all blue in the face.

George was frightened.

Fortunately the men had heard the noise. They came rushing to the cage and got the bugle out of the ostrich's throat just in time.

The director was very angry with George. "We cannot use little monkeys who don't do as they are told," he said. "Of course you cannot take part in the show now. We will have to send you home."

George had to sit on a bench all by himself and nobody even looked at him. He was terribly sorry for what he had done but now it was too late. He had spoiled everything.

Meanwhile the ostrich, always hungry, had got hold of a string dangling near his cage. This happened to be the string which held the door to the cage of the baby bear. As the ostrich nibbled at it the door opened — and the baby bear got out.

He ran away as fast as
he could and made straight
for a high tree near the camp.

Nobody had seen it but
George—and George was not
supposed to leave his bench.
But this was an emergency,

so he jumped up, grabbed the bugle, and blew as loud as he

could. Then he rushed

to his bicycle.

The men had
heard the alarm
and thought at first
that George had
been naughty again.
But when they saw
the empty cage and
the ostrich nibbling
at the string, they knew
what had happened.

George raced toward the tree,
far ahead of the men.

By now the bear had climbed
quite high—and this was dangerous
because little bears can
climb up a tree easily
but coming down
is much harder;

they may fall
and get hurt.
The men were worried.
They did not know how
to get him down safely.
But George had his plan:

with the bag over his shoulder he went up the tree as fast
as only a monkey can, and when he reached the baby bear

he put him
in his bag
and carefully
let him down
so that the men
could safely
catch him.

40

Everybody cheered when George had come down from the tree. "You are a brave little monkey," said the director, "you saved the baby bear's life. Now you'll get your coat back and of course you may ride your bike and play the bugle in the show."

Finally the show was on. The
and how surprised they were
right in the middle of it!
and also the man

42

whole town had come to see it,
to discover George on his bike
The newsboy was there, too,
with the yellow hat

43

who had been looking for George everywhere and was happy to have found him at last. The newsboy was glad to have his bag again, and the people from the other side of the street whose papers George had made into boats were not angry with him any more.

George!

When the time had come for George to say goodbye,
the director let him keep the coat and the cap and the bugle.
And then George and his friend got into the car and went . . .

good Night!